WHAT your
Mama NEVER
Told you

WHAT YouR MaMa NEVER, ToLD YoU

TRue STorieS AbouT Sex and Love

Edited by
Tara Roberts

AN IMPRINT OF HOUGHTON MIFFLIN COMPANY
Boston 2007

Library of Congress Cataloging-in-Publication Data

What your mama never told you : true stories about sex and love / edited by Tara
Roberts.
  p. cm.
 ISBN-13: 978-0-618-64636-4 (pbk. : alk. paper)
 ISBN-10: 0-618-64636-1 (pbk. : alk. paper)
 1. African American teenage girls—Sexual behavior—Case studies. 2. African
American teenage girls—Psychology. 3. African American teenage girls—Biography.
I. Roberts, Tara.
 HQ27.5.W45 2006
 306.7089'96073—dc22

                                                                          2006004